A Note to Parents and Caregivers:

Read-it! Readers are for children who are just starting on the amazing road to reading. These beautiful books support both the acquisition of reading skills and the love of books.

The PURPLE LEVEL presents basic topics and objects using high frequency words and simple language patterns.

The RED LEVEL presents familiar topics using common words and repeating sentence patterns.

The BLUE LEVEL presents new ideas using a larger vocabulary and varied sentence structure.

The YELLOW LEVEL presents more challenging ideas, a broad vocabulary, and wide variety in sentence structure.

The GREEN LEVEL presents more complex ideas, an extended vocabulary range, and expanded language structures.

The ORANGE LEVEL presents a wide range of ideas and concepts using challenging vocabulary and complex language structures.

When sharing a book with your child, read in short stretches, pausing often to talk about the pictures. Have your child turn the pages and point to the pictures and familiar words. And be sure to reread favorite stories or parts of stories.

There is no right or wrong way to share books with children. Find time to read with your child, and pass on the legacy of literacy.

Adria F. Klein, Ph.D.
Professor Emeritus
California State University
San Bernardino, California

For Conner Blaukat—J.K.

Editor: Nick Healy
Designer: Joe Anderson
Page Production: Brandie E. Shoemaker
Creative Director: Keith Griffin
Editorial Director: Carol Jones
The illustrations in this book were created digitally.

Picture Window Books
5115 Excelsior Boulevard
Suite 232
Minneapolis, MN 55416
877-845-8392
www.picturewindowbooks.com

Printed in the United States of America.

Library of Congress Cataloging-in-Publication Data
Kalz, Jill.
Boy who loved trains / by Jill Kalz ; illustrated by Sahin Erkocak.
p. cm. — (Read-it! readers)
Summary: Conner loves trains so much that the only thing he ever says is "Woo! Woo!"
until he opens a special gift one Christmas Day.
ISBN-13: 978-1-4048-2401-0 (hardcover)
ISBN-10: 1-4048-2401-4 (hardcover)
[1. Railroads—Trains—Fiction. 2. Christmas—Fiction.] I. Erkocak, Sahin, ill. II.
Title. III. Series.
PZ7.K12655Boy 2007
[E]—dc22   2006009191

The Boy Who Loved Trains

by Jill Kalz
illustrated by Sahin Erkocak

Special thanks to our advisers for their expertise:

Adria F. Klein, Ph.D.
Professor Emeritus, California State University
San Bernardino, California

Susan Kesselring, M.A.
Literacy Educator
Rosemount–Apple Valley–Eagan (Minnesota) School District

PICTURE WINDOW BOOKS
Minneapolis, Minnesota

Conner was a little boy who said only one word: "Woo!" But he always said it twice: "Woo! Woo!"

Conner loved trains.

ains chugged across his walls. They puffed round his bed. They whistled on his shirt and ven on his pants.

One special morning, Conner's mom asked, "Would you like peanut butter on your toast? How about grape or apple jelly?"

Conner said, "Woo! Woo!"

9

In the afternoon, Conner's dad asked,
"Would you like to help me shovel snow?"

Conner said, "Woo! Woo!"

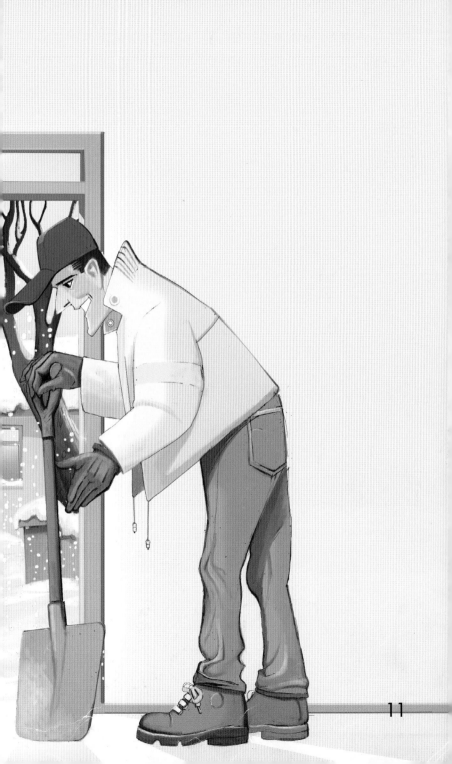

11

Just before dinnertime, the doorbell rang. Conner's grandma and grandpa walked in. They carried presents. So did Aunt Sally. She smelled like peppermint candy.

13

The biggest present was for Conner. "What do you think it is?" Aunt Sally asked.

Conner said, "Woo! Woo!"

Was it a train sleeping bag or a new train table? Was it a train toy box? Was it a giant stuffed train?

17

Conner tore off the bows and ribbons. He ripped the shiny paper.

Aunt Sally threw up her hands. "It's a race car!" she exclaimed.

Now Conner is a little boy who says a brand-new word. But he always says it twice: "Vroom! Vroom!"

More *Read-it!* Readers

Bright pictures and fun stories help you practice your reading skills. Look for more books at your level.

The Best Lunch 1-4048-1578-3
Car Shopping 1-4048-2406-5
Clinks the Robot 1-4048-1579-1
Firefly Summer 1-4048-2397-2
The Flying Fish 1-4048-2410-3
Flynn Flies High 1-4048-0563-X
Freddie's Fears 1-4048-0056-5
Loop, Swoop, and Pull! 1-4048-1611-9
Megan Has to Move 1-4048-1613-5
Moo! 1-4048-0643-1
My Favorite Monster 1-4048-1029-3
Paulette's Friend 1-4048-2398-0
Pippin's Big Jump 1-4048-0555-9
Pony Party 1-4048-1612-7
Rudy Helps Out 1-4048-2420-0
The Snow Dance 1-4048-2421-9
Sounds Like Fun 1-4048-0649-0
The Ticket 1-4048-2423-5
Tired of Waiting 1-4048-0650-4
Tuckerbean in the Kitchen 1-4048-2402-2
Whose Birthday Is It? 1-4048-0554-0

Looking for a specific title or level? A complete list of *Read-it!* Readers is available on our Web site:
www.picturewindowbooks.com